About the author

Peter Robson was educated in England. He went to London University to take a degree in engineering. He worked at Vickers Armstrongs in Newcastle, and later as an engineer on a ship, which travelled between Africa and Europe. He worked at Ford Motor Company as a design and test engineer.

Later he worked at an engineering research company in Sweden. When this job unfortunately finished, because of the employing company's economic problems, he started his own company as a toolmaker.

WHILE YOU ARE WAITING STORIES

Peter Robson

WHILE YOU ARE WAITING STORIES

Vanguard Press

VANGUARD PAPERBACK

© Copyright 2016
Peter Robson

The right of Peter Robson to be identified as author of
this work has been asserted by him in accordance with the
Copyright, Designs and Patents Act 1988.

All Rights Reserved

No reproduction, copy or transmission of this publication
may be made without written permission.
No paragraph of this publication may be reproduced,
copied or transmitted save with the written permission of the
publisher, or in accordance with the provisions
of the Copyright Act 1956 (as amended).

Any person who commits any unauthorised act in relation to
this publication may be liable to criminal
prosecution and civil claims for damages.

A CIP catalogue record for this title is
available from the British Library.

ISBN   9781784651763

*Vanguard Press is an imprint of
Pegasus Elliot MacKenzie Publishers Ltd.*
www.pegasuspublishers.com

First Published in 2016

**Vanguard Press
Sheraton House   Castle Park
Cambridge   England**

Printed & Bound in Great Britain

This is dedicated to all the kind, reliable workmates I have known.

THE ARTIST

There are many galleries around the world, showing works of modern art. Visitors often leave with many questions in mind: what were the artists thinking when they produced their pictures? What training did the artists have? How do the artists live? And suchlike. This is the story of the artist Jack Bullock, and it tries to answer some of these questions.

Jack was born in Huddersfield in 1952. He was educated at Blackgate Secondary Modern School. From sixteen he served an apprenticeship with a local engineering company. When he was twenty-two he joined the Merchant Navy as an engineer. He and his wife Monica met in 1979, when his ship was in Gothenburg loading Volvo cars for transport to America. Monica was employed as a driver, loading cars onto the ship. Jack had found Gothenburg boring, and was earning overtime pay helping the deck crew. He and Monica met in the ship's canteen and during this meeting Monica suggested that they could explore Gothenburg together and she could show him interesting pubs and suchlike. They married a year afterwards, Jack gave up his seagoing work and they moved to Monica's family home near Husqvarna.

The story is based on knowledge from a close friendship with Jack and his wife Monica and some interviews with acquaintances when necessary. Jack had little formal training as an artist. His natural ability came to the fore after his first work was exhibited in Jönköping, Sweden, in 1986. This story starts from when Jack and Monica first started living together in Sweden.

The value of a U.S. dollar to the Swedish kronor has varied from 1:14 to 1:7.5. An easy guide for this story is to take 1 dollar:10 kronor.

CHAPTER 1

It was a summer evening in June, and Jack and Monica were sitting on the balcony at home. There was nothing much on the television, as was quite usual in Sweden during the summer.

Monica was reading the advertisements in the local paper when she suddenly started.

"Gosh! We must visit the Vernissage at the town hall in Jönköping. We can visit it after we have been shopping on Saturday."

"Visit the what? What did you say?" Jack answered.

"The Vernissage. It's an exhibition of art works by local artists, and in fact anyone in the county. We've missed the exhibition for the past three years."

Jack contemplated this, and remembered the excuse that he had used last year – visiting Monica's aunt – and the excuse the year before – painting the house. It was difficult to find an excuse now at such short notice, but maybe the visit could be for a limited time.

"We'd better make it a short visit, otherwise the frozen things we buy will thaw out."

Jack's relief was short lived.

"Oh, they'll be OK. I can take the plastic cold box and some ice blocks from the freezer," Monica answered.

After completing the shopping, which took longer than expected, they parked their old Volkswagen in a shady spot and took a short walk to the town hall. The Vernissage was on the first floor and there were maybe a dozen other visitors. After half an hour they had looked at about fifty exhibits in a long hall. There were a few paintings where one could see immediately what they were trying to represent, others were partially abstract and many completely abstract, being single coloured squares and suchlike.

There were some that looked like asphalt with some white lines. Obviously they were sophisticated and designed to provoke thought. Even the titles provoked thought. What did 'reconstituted' and 'reclaimed' really mean? Other titles sprang to Jack's mind.

Jack looked through an open door and saw there was another room full of artworks and, oh heavens, through an archway he could see a third room.

There were four chairs at the end of this room and Jack spotted one being vacated. He moved quickly, beating another younger man by three metres.

Monica moved over and stood in front of him.

"This is a load of crap," was Jack's comment.

Monica set her mouth.

"Many people are interested in art – look at the number of exhibits and the visitors. You sit here and I'll meet you again in about half an hour."

Jack looked at the three other men sitting on the chairs, one of whom had fallen asleep with his mouth open. He wished that he had brought a book.

The half hour turned into an hour, but after that Jack and Monica were on their way home. The exhibition came up again in their conversation.

"So you didn't like it?" Monica asked.

"To be honest, I think that they've hung up anything they could get their hands on."

"You do remember that I have tried for the last two years to get one of my paintings accepted by the city council." Monica was somewhat annoyed. She continued, "If you think it is that easy, then you paint a picture and send it in to them."

Jack thought about this for a while. If he did send in a picture and it was accepted, then not only would he have won the argument but he would have a very logical argument for avoiding going to any further exhibitions – why waste your free time looking at such things? Those simple asphalt paintings he had seen – he had asphalted the garage roof in an afternoon last month. Asphalting a square metre of plate to make a picture could not take more than twenty minutes. And anyway, if his painting was not accepted, it was no great loss.

"OK, I'll do a painting."

Monica smiled, "I knew you might. Going to an exhibition is actually stimulating, even if you don't realise it at the time."

Monica was pleased. She had always hoped that Jack would be more interested in paintings and art. She said that she would send in at least two of her paintings. She knew it would be just great when they both had a common interest.

The afternoon finished in agreement, and Jack and Monica were home within a quarter of an hour.

CHAPTER 2

Jack and Monica's home was a two storey wooden house built in 1932, in a village outside of Husqvarna. There was a large garden and a separate wooden garage. Monica's mother had lived in the house until she died three years earlier. With such a house there were always repairs waiting to be carried out, or perhaps modifications required, or painting needed. The garden also required time; it was mostly a large lawn with fruit trees, but the lawn had to be mowed and the trees pruned. A tractor-mower was on the list of purchases when Jack and Monica had money to spare.

Jack was an energetic man. He cycled to work at the local saw mill, was a trainer for young boys at the local football club and tried to do everything possible around the home himself: painting, repairs, the garden, and even servicing the car. There were two children, these being Monica's from her previous marriage – a girl of thirteen and a boy of eleven. Sometimes the children helped, perhaps in the garden, but mostly they ensured that Jack and Monica had little time over for themselves.

Monica worked at a nursery school three days a week. The two free days gave her time, when the children were in school, for some painting – first with watercolours, then with pastels, and finally with oil paints.

Time continued, Christmas came and went, presents were given and received. By March, Monica had painted three pictures ready to be sent in to Jönköping council. Jack however, had given little thought to his promise to paint a picture. At the end of March there was an article in the local paper about the coming exhibition – pictures were to be submitted by the fourteenth of April. It was Monica who read the article in the local paper and reminded Jack of his promise to do a painting.

"OK," was Jack's grunted reply. He regretted having said he would do a painting – so many other things to do. He remembered an article in a popular magazine in the library that had revealed that artists had tried just about everything. Paint had been splashed on, sprayed on, dripped, and wiped on. Every kind of paint had been tried, including asphalt. At this time the painting seemed much less important than organising the junior league football match on Saturday.

However the next evening Jack was to be found in the garage trying to find the asphalt he had used on the roof. There was a little left and he also found some under sealer he had used on the Volkswagen.

The next day he collected a square metre of plate from the local roofing company, and set to work in the garage. Painting turned out to be a messy business. He worked with the plate on the garage floor. He thought of a complete background of asphalt, some splodges of under sealer to give it 'texture', and then a few white lines. It would look similar to something he had seen at the Vernissage with a price tag of ten thousand kronor. The painting took nearly two hours, rather than the twenty minutes he had at first estimated.

The next few evenings he went to look at his artwork. By the fourth evening he realised that it was not going to dry in time, certainly not by the fourteenth. It was cold in the garage. Jack set up a fan heater to blow over the painting and hopefully drive off some of the remaining solvents. He turned off the light and stepped over the edge of the painting as he was leaving. It was then that it happened. He stepped on the upturned lid of the under sealer tin and his foot went from under him. He sat down on his painting.

Jack groaned. It was difficult getting up but anger helped his efforts. One elbow had gone down on his picture too, and his boiler suit was more or less ruined – what luck that he had been wearing it!

He turned the light on and looked at his 'picture'. It was certainly not as he had planned it. But was the damage of great consequence? It had never been a serious project to start with. There was a flat round area where his behind had landed, surrounded by a ring of tiny up-reaching asphalt fingers. His elbow had given a similar smaller elongated impression. What to do? He spent the next quarter of an hour trying to clean his boiler suit with thinners and considered the matter. The only answer was to get the picture to dry and then just take it in to Jönköping.

Jack told Monica about the accident. They went to the garage and Monica regarded it with amusement.

"You'll have to sign it too," she started to giggle.

Jack was tired of the whole painting project and wrote 'Bollocks' at the bottom with white paint. 'Bollocks' had often been his nickname in his earlier life, and it seemed so very suitable now. The 's' ran off the edge of the plate.

"You cannot just write that. Give it your full name, like all artists."

Jack added 'Jack' in front. "And that's it," Jack finalised.

It took another two nights for the painting to dry with the fan heater running all night. Jack's 'painting' and three of Monica's were delivered to Jönköping town hall on the Friday evening. It took the whole of the evening; driving there, having them registered and getting reference numbers. Jack then forgot all about the painting and concentrated on the football matches for his team of eleven year olds.

CHAPTER 3

After five weeks a letter arrived from Jönköping's council saying that two of Monica's paintings had been accepted and even Jack's. The result was excitement and considerable pride from Monica. She was so pleased and laughed and congratulated Jack. Jack could only admit that he did now have some interest – if only the visit did not have to be as long as last year.

Jack and Monica made a visit that lasted nearly two hours. Jack's interest dwindled after he had seen his own painting and a few others, but this time he took a book with him and he found an early place on a chair. Monica visited the exhibition twice more herself during the three weeks it was open.

Now the remarkable thing was that art experts, who did understand, decided that Jack's painting should be bought by Jönköping's council, this after the director of the Modern Museum in Stockholm had expressed an interest in it. He had stopped by Jönköping on his way from Stockholm to Göteborg. It was clear that Jack's painting was different and new, and the impressions in the asphalt and under sealer could lead to many interpretations for the imaginative mind. As the director of the Modern Museum said, it gave an impression of action and energy. It stood out among the other paintings. The ten thousand kronor that Jack had set as a fantasy price was so gratefully accepted, and was the basis for Jack and Monica buying a new tractor-mower.

Jack's amazement and self-justification knew no bounds when the director of the exhibition in Jönköping later telephoned to ask whether he had another painting available that the Modern Museum in Stockholm would be interested in buying. How long did it take to do a painting? Had it been difficult to form the impressions? With honesty Jack could say that the impressions had been somewhat difficult, and the paintings did take many hours to finish – he did not mention that ninety-five percent of the time was taken up by trying to get the thing to dry. And certainly for ten thousand kronor he could arrange for another painting.

Jack's artistic career progressed inexorably. The director of the Hamburger Kunsthalle bought a picture after having seen Jack's second in the Modern Museum in Stockholm. All were made by the same process. Jack kept, what Monica now called his 'lucky' boiler suit, to perform the impressions. The prices of his pictures quite naturally rose, price rises of twenty-five percent or sometimes even fifty percent seemed to be acceptable. Of course the asphalt was always more or less the same, but all makes of under sealer were tried, and lines were drawn using various colours, making each picture quite individual. He also varied his method of making the impressions: sometimes one, sometimes several, depending on the size of the plate he was working on. He sometimes got up slowly, sometimes quickly. On one or two he even did a little spin with his feet in the air, which would have done credit to a gymnast.

One picture was accidentally run over by Monica pushing a wheelbarrow. The wheel made a clear pattern across the upper corner of this picture, which was a four square metre model.

Jack had discovered that the value of his pictures was almost directly proportional to their size, but the work involved in producing them was almost the same, the cost of the raw materials being irrelevant. Monica managed to avoid getting her feet on the picture but the barrow tipped over after reaching the edge, and the last part of the wheel track was distinctly wobbly. Monica was devastated. She had begun to realise that Jack was a gifted artist. However Jack said he would keep the picture as it was. The wheel track was an interesting extra. It was exhibited in a well-known gallery. Viking Automobile Industries bought it, or to more correct, their art consultant did.

Evert Haag, the chairman of Viking Industries, was very busy as always, however he thought it necessary to make a quick telephone call to the art consultant after this latest purchase had been delivered to his office. He had thought that a Jackson Pollock painting would brighten up the board room with its beautiful streams of colours. What he had received was not going to brighten up anything.

He was used to direct questions and concise answers.

"Is this latest painting I've received a Jackson Pollock or not?"

He was told by the art consultant that it was not a Jackson Pollock but a Jack Bullock, an excellent investment by an up-and-coming artist whose works had been purchased by several galleries, and also the picture had an industrial motif.

Evert Haag made a noncommittal noise and put the receiver down. It was he who had approved the two hundred and forty thousand kronor to purchase the picture; not very much, but on the other hand there was a mistake somewhere about the name of the artist. He did not make mistakes, and if he did, he did not admit them, even to himself.

He looked at the painting, which had been propped against the wall until he decided where it should be hung. Was that tyre track an industrial motif? Huh! The plate was probably not even galvanised and would rust at the back with time. He got up and checked it. No, it was not galvanised and it was already starting to rust.

He made a quick telephone call to have the picture removed to somewhere else and not the board room, and hung very securely high up.

If anyone brushed against it, it would probably ruin their suit, and if it ever fell down it could kill people.

That being decided, he returned to work. But he could not get the picture out of his mind. It was disturbing; it called into question the values of today's society, and indeed the modern view of investment and economy. He was devoting almost every second of his waking hours to ensuring that Viking stayed ahead in a very competitive industry. He thought of the finesse and requirements of a modern automobile, and here was a piece of painted plate sold for the same price. Yes, one could buy an excellent family car for that money.

CHAPTER 4

Jack and Monica had by this time made investments themselves. A new house had been bought, with a beautiful view over a lake. On the basis of his artistic talents, Jack had even got planning permission for a large studio with panoramic windows. The house was completed and the studio almost so.

"Oh this is just wonderful," said Monica. She was planning the furniture for their new house.

Jack pointed out that at present their economy was somewhat stretched. But Monica did not worry; she knew now that Jack was a very talented artist and that any money problems would solve themselves with time.

A Russian businessman living in Helsinki had bought two of Jack's paintings as an investment. On a visit to St. Petersburg he suffered an untimely death by machine gun fire, and this resulted in the paintings being sent to Christie's to be auctioned. They were both the same size but had different colours splashed on.

The auctioneer at Christie's had decided to pronounce Jack's name as Bow-lock. Nobody could possibly be called Bollock, even if they did live in Scandinavia, and it was of vital importance that an air of seriousness was preserved during the auction. This would have been successful if a Frenchman had not asked at the start of the auction, if the pictures should not be sold as a pair. Some people were forced to check whether their shoe laces were fastened, and one lady made an exit chewing her handkerchief.

The sale was in fact very successful, thanks to the telephone bidding. The first picture was sold for fifty-three thousand dollars and the second reached fifty thousand dollars with two bidders remaining. There was Karl Spetch, a property dealer from California, and Sheik Al Kasily from Oman. Sheik Al Kasily won the bidding with an offer of fifty-five thousand dollars.

Jack and Monica were delighted by the prices that the pictures were fetching. Of course the Swedish tax system took a voracious bite but, because of the low production costs, Jack and Monica's finances were soon in a very good state.

The studio in the grounds of their new house was now completed. Jack was away for a few days in Geneva and Monica had some friends round for coffee. She liked showing them around – the new house, the furnishings, the garden and also Jack's new studio. But she did not let them into the studio without Jack being there. She held the door half open and let them look in. It was an impressive place with the wide windows looking out over the lake. There was a smell of new wood so typical of new Swedish wooden houses. Whiskers the cat had followed along too. He was very interested in the new studio and, while the door was half open and all attention was being directed at the view, he made a quick dart inside. Monica closed the door behind him.

Whiskers made a thorough investigation of this new place. He marked it out as his territory, rubbing his head against furniture legs and suchlike.

He was not missed for the first day. Poor Whiskers needed to get out. He was hungry and there was a call of nature that was becoming desperate. He looked around for a place where a little pile could be deposited unnoticed. There was no such place. Being a fastidious cat, he chose what he thought was a piece of road. It was one of Jack's pictures which had been left on the floor to dry. He left a little pile on the lower left hand corner.

Whiskers was found next day by Monica, who made a great fuss of him.

Jack had a very successful four day trip to Geneva. One of his works was now installed in the Museum of Modern Art there. On the way home he bought the full ration of wine, beer and spirits allowed into Sweden.

Unfortunately he strained his back carrying this, together with his other bags, from the airport to his car.

He told Monica all about his successful trip on returning home. She glowed with pride. Next day he worked in his studio with renewed enthusiasm. The pain in his back was a problem, however he worked on, fortified by a glass or two of the Napoleon brandy he had brought back. He used a long brush to apply the final coat to his latest work. The painting was on the floor and the long brush saved him from bending down too much. He did notice a bump or little pile in the corner but it was already covered in the same instant. He gave it a second glance. The Napoleon brandy gave him a happy-go-lucky attitude. "So what," he said. He gave it an extra coat of asphalt and forgot about it.

CHAPTER 5

Karl Spetch, however, had not forgotten about having missed buying the Pollock at Christie's. A telephone call from an art dealer had revealed that another was for sale at a well-known dealer's in London. What luck! Art was as good an investment as property, and there was not as much paperwork, lawyers, or taxes involved.

Karl telephoned directory enquiries, rang the art dealer, hesitated a few seconds and bought the painting. It was wonderful how effective a visa card was when making an international purchase, and the painting was slightly cheaper than the one he had tried to buy at Christie's.

The painting was delivered three weeks later by DHL, arriving in a well-constructed wooden crate. Should he open the crate on the lawn in front of the house? No! With considerable effort he managed to get the crate onto the door mat and drag the whole lot into his study. A crowbar was fetched from the garage. The people who made the crate took pride in their work and were artists in their way too.

At last the planks were loosened and nails drawn out. He could lift out the painting, which had a simple wooden frame around it with linen sheet coverings. Karl removed the linen sheets. A black surface was revealed. Was this the back or the front?

It took nearly ten minutes for Karl to appreciate the situation. One side was black with a few simple lines and the other side was a simple steel plate with a little rust in places. This was no Jackson Pollock. His hands quivered with anguish as he lifted the art work onto his desk to view it in a better light. The bottom corner dragged against the edge of his desk and a protrusion loosened. The loose piece fell onto the carpet.

Karl twisted the painting around so that it was supported by the wall. No! This was not a Jackson Pollock. One of London's old established art dealers, my arse! He would start by ringing them immediately – if they were still in business. He began a desperate search for the letter and receipt he had been sent when he bought the 'painting'.

Prince the black labrador was four years old and a sensible and well balanced dog. He had followed Karl into the study in the morning when the crate had been dragged in. It was beyond his ability to grasp why such a simple heavy object must be dragged immediately into the study, but humans often did strange things. It was nearly midday and Prince lay on his rug and contemplated his evening meal.

Suddenly he realised that something was wrong. There was a smell that should not be there. There was a nasty smell of new road, but something else too – could some other animal, have marked his territory with a shit? He sniffed again, and was up in a flash. This was serious. He moved quickly, following the source of the smell. It was in the very centre of his territory, on the floor beside the boss's desk. He moved closer to make a complete odour identification.

Karl Spetch was gripped with rage. He'd been stung. Taken in – and him with all his experience of the world! Not only that, but by an Englishman too, a limey jerk. Those toffee-nosed limey jerks! If they could get the marbles out of their mouths, maybe they could talk English like everyone else. Boy, had he been sold a load of shit. He looked up from his desk and saw Prince's tail.

He stood up and saw that Prince was interested in the piece that had been knocked off the picture. He twisted his desk lamp around so that it shone onto the carpet, and joined Prince on his hands and knees to examine the piece on the carpet. Karl's sense of smell gave him little guidance but if his eyes were to be believed this was a piece of turd encased in asphalt. It could not be – but judging from Prince's interest it must be. "Incredible." He felt cold and his stomach had been replaced by a large lump of lead.

He looked at Prince who simultaneously returned the look;

their eyes were only twenty centimetres apart. Prince decided that a good series of barks at the object on the carpet was the right and proper thing to do.

Karl was too shocked to tell Prince to be quiet. He just got up and returned to his desk. He continued the desperate search for the letter and receipt he had been sent when he purchased the picture. He must have put them in a drawer somewhere. There they were!

MAYFAIR FINE ARTS GALLERY, owned by Algernon St. John Villiers.

His telephone call was unanswered since it was after seven p.m. in London. "St. Bastard Villiers," Karl talked to himself, as he waited for directory enquiries to find the home number. When he received the number he rang but there was no answer. He rang again and let the telephone ring. When he was about to replace the receiver there was a reply.

"Algernon St. John Villiers."

"This is Karl Spetch ringing from California to tell you that I am going to sue you for everything that you have got. That 'Jackson Pollock' that you sent me is a load of shit, and when I say shit I mean shit."

Algernon St. John Villiers was taken aback, but after years of experience he remained perfectly calm. Also it was obvious that he was dealing with a complete idiot.

"I have never sold a Jackson Pollock in my life. It is a pleasure that yet awaits me one lucky day, I hope."

Algernon had often found that a little light conversation was helpful in such circumstances. In this case it was not helpful.

"Listen to me, you little bastard. I paid you fifty-two

thousand bucks and you have sent me a piece of plate with bits of shit on it. One of the filthy bits has even fallen off, and this is supposed to be a Jackson Pollock."

Algernon was now very sure that he was dealing with an idiot, and not only that but a complete Philistine too.

"What I sent you was a Jack Bollock, a guaranteed genuine example of the artist's work. Indeed, may I suggest that you look at the bill of sale which was sent to you. In addition, I can point out to you that any damage whatsoever to the picture will seriously decrease its value."

Karl looked at the bill of sale. It was a Jack Bollock he had bought. Algernon St. John Villiers was still talking on the telephone but he did not hear him. He just put the receiver down.

He knew there was only one thing to do. "Find another sucker," he said to himself.

But first the art work had to be repaired. He put the picture flat on his desk and picked up the asphalted turd in a tissue paper. He set to work to replace it using office glue.

Prince was completely baffled. His barks of warning and frustration were ignored. He had been told to 'shut up' a couple of times. He remembered when he was a pup and had left a little deposit near the door (very reasonable he had thought) and all the fuss that had been made about that.

Human beings were a complete mystery. He sat back and watched. His ears had been erect so long with all his thinking, that the muscles on the back of his head ached with cramp. He shook his head vigorously and went to lie on his mat.

His amazement increased when the boss hung the picture on the wall. He moved over and stood on his back legs to give a sniff check. Perhaps it had been changed in a mysterious way that humans could fix. No! The offending bit was still there all right; it was cat he was sure of that, and fed on tinned cat food if he was not mistaken. No wild stray cat. The boss noticed him and shouted at him to get away. He sounded very angry.

Back on his mat Prince sat down to think again. It was very clear what he had always suspected, that human beings had no sense of smell. Drat! Thinking made his ears stick up and gave him that cramp on the top of his head. He shook his head. Now there was a tickle in his ear. He gave his left ear a good scratch with his hind leg. It was in the middle of this scratch that everything suddenly became clear to him. His hind leg stopped in mid scratch and fell slowly to the mat.

Not only did humans have no sense of smell but they had no effective senses at all!

Taste and food – the time they took to eat their food, they hardly seemed to like it. The smallest ones, the children, were worst. They did not seem to know what eating was. He thought of his pal Rex, the two year old rottweiler up the road. He could really show people how to eat.

Their sense of hearing was hopeless. They did not hear the gate. They did not hear people coming up the path. They did not hear if people were knocking on the door and they needed that ringing bell thing.

When they met they hardly made contact, just touched paws for a short time, and then carried on as usual. If one of his friends arrived there were real greetings – jumping on each other, and possibly a race to see who was fastest.

Yes, human beings were totally insensitive, and that was why they hung shit on the wall. Prince felt a glow of contentment flooding through his body – he had sorted out one of life's mysteries. He lay down and soon fell asleep. He dreamt that Rex had come for a visit, and his legs twitched as he ran in his sleep.

Funny animals dogs, Karl thought when looked up from his desk and saw Prince. I wonder if they have thoughts like we do. He returned to his urgent work evaluating possible investments for his dollars, and also to the problem of 'finding another sucker'.

CHAPTER 6

Jack and Monica had so many dollars by now, that they decided a holiday home was in order. They had considered Spain, Greece, Florida, and even the West Indies. That summer when the children were away (their daughter being nineteen now was living with her boyfriend, and their son was staying with Jack's parents in England) they had made a visit to Antigua. It was beautiful and the beaches glorious, however after having been ripped off by taxi drivers and every other restaurant, and all to Bob Marley music, they decided to look elsewhere. While returning across the United States by car they stayed for a week outside Los Angeles.

They made enquiries at various house agents and as a result of doing so met Sam Jenkins. Sam, known as 'Turbo Mouth' to his associates and few friends, was Karl Spetch's sales manager. It took only two days for Sam to sell them the apartment that he had been trying to get rid of for nearly a year. The apartment overlooked the beach. It was large, had a fine balcony and all fittings.

"Many artists live around here," he had told Jack, and Jack had responded with genuine interest,

"Gosh! Is that so? I'd like to meet people like that."

Jack and Monica paid the asking price for the apartment, much to Sam's delight and indeed astonishment.

Unfortunately Jack and Monica soon found the disadvantages. The nearby shops and businesses seemed to be open all night, sand blew in everywhere if the balcony door was left open. The only artists they met were salesmen in the local shops, who were so clever at selling, that Jack soon had many cameras, lenses, telescopes, satellite receivers for caravans and suchlike that he did not know where to put them all.

The truth is that Jack really wanted to be in an area with artists. He wanted to know how and why his pictures were appreciated. He understood why directors of modern museums bought them. They looked quite reasonable in such museums, and museum directors were quite special people, and it had been easy to learn how to make appropriate talk when he discussed art with them. But he wanted to know how other artists, and indeed ordinary people who bought his pictures, evaluated them. Deep inside he did not really understand it.

He woke up at night sometimes and started to think about it and had difficulty in getting to sleep again. He sometimes thought he had entered a dream world where nothing was real. Maybe he would wake up one day and find he was back at his job at the saw mill.

The few times he had talked to 'normal people' about his paintings he had received no guidance at all. Some had laughed, a few had been rude, and one had been quite threatening. He had talked to Monica and told her that under no circumstances were they to reveal his work as an artist, unless they knew the people very well.

Karl Spetch was delighted when Sam Jenkins rang to tell him that the apartment in the Swales district was sold. And not only that, but sold at the original asking price.

"Who the hell bought it?"

Sam replied that it was a couple from Europe somewhere.

"They talked with a funny accent – Swedes I think they said. Oh yes, the guy said he came from England to start with. Plenty of money anyway. I gave them the story of the area being full of artists, and they seemed really interested in art and artists."

"Send me a fax with their names and find their telephone number too."

Karl was a born opportunist and never missed a chance. Finding another sucker was not going to be easy, but this was a possibility, and as such was not to be missed.

Karl was president of the local Art Society. It befitted a serious art collector such as himself, and he had been prepared to offer the time that the presidency required. The next monthly meeting was to be held in his house, and he sent Jack and Monica an invitation. Two days after the invitation was delivered he telephoned them, to make the invitation more personal, and indeed to make sure that they came.

Monica answered the telephone. She was delighted that he had rung to confirm the invitation – but how had he found their names and address to know to invite them?

"Oh, the Art Society gets a list of all new residents to the area, and people from Europe are of interest to the society since there are so many European artists," Karl lied.

No, he was not an artist himself, but a property developer, and was president of the local Art Society.

He gave Monica clear instructions as to how to drive to his house, since Jack and Monica now had a hire car, and said that he looked forward very much to meeting them.

Jack and Monica discussed the invitation; they were so pleased to make contact with a friendly American instead of apartment salesmen and shop sales people. And an invitation to a local art society would indeed be interesting.

Truth to tell, the disappointment with the apartment was increasing with time. The area was not at all what they had been led to expect. Poor Monica had had her handbag stolen, and the noise in the evenings from cars and motorcycles was not at all what they wanted, least of all in a holiday home. It was true that the apartment had all modern conveniences, however with the balcony door having to be kept shut, and the air conditioner being of limited capacity and questionable reliability, a holiday atmosphere was hard to maintain.

They had learned that in America the dollar was king and salesmen were ruthless.

"Perhaps we can find another sucker to buy this place," was Jack's bitter comment when the air conditioner went on strike for the second time, just before they were about to go to bed.

"That man Spetch who rang us is a property dealer," Monica replied. "Maybe we can ask his advice? He might even be interested in buying it. And he's American. I've got a whole load of American sales talk just ready on the end of my tongue."

The meeting of the Art Society took place on a Saturday afternoon. Karl had thirty-two paintings, about half of which were in his study. Over fifty people came to the meeting – it was a very social gathering.

Karl was pleased to see most of the visitors. The priest and the Methodist minister made him feel uncomfortable, but this was soon forgotten as he met Jack and Monica. Among the other guests he paid them special attention.

How did they like America? What did Jack do?

Jack replied that he was a manufacturer of oil products.

How did he invest his money?

Jack said he never gave investments much thought, however he had bought a holiday home which one could regard as an investment.

"You're right there," was Karl's reply.

Monica seized the opportunity to break into the conversation and said that they must sell it because of family problems at home in Sweden. Would Karl be interested in buying it?

This was not at all what Karl wanted but it was vital to stay friendly. He asked about the apartment.

This was all that Monica needed. She repeated all the sales talk that Sam 'Turbo Mouth' Jenkins had given her, with extra embellishments of her own. Karl was surprised by this glowing report and, to maintain their friendship, he agreed to look at the apartment.

Actually, after listening to Monica's description he started to feel in good humour. No, he hadn't cheated people, he had given them good value for money. He started to wonder if Sam Jenkins was not selling things too cheaply. He would have a word with Sam. In the meantime he found himself smiling at the priest and enjoying having a chat with the minister. But buy back the apartment? That was not at all in his plans.

As the party moved into his study he took Jack by the elbow

and steered him over to the Jack Bullock painting.

"Here's a great artwork. Have you ever come across Bullock's work before?"

Jack and Monica looked at each other, but before they could reply Karl continued.

"Yes, a great picture. When I look at this it clears my mind and calms me down. I think of deep space and primeval energy, and how small we human beings are."

Monica glowed with pride, and said yes, it really was very special. Jack was speechless, not least because he had caught sight of Whisker's asphalted turd.

"Aw, you're looking at the protrusion there. That always reminds me that there is something unexpected in life. It's like the first pulse of energy at the beginning of the universe."

Jack made some sort of noise. Karl decided to concentrate his sales talk on Monica; this guy Jack was some sort of dumb mutt.

"Now this picture has been a great investment. It's increased in value by at least ten percent during the short time I've had it."

He continued telling Monica how he might – just might – consider selling it if the land deal he had been after for years, near Sacramento, turned up.

Monica hung onto his every word, and with smiles. She was so pleased and proud. And she would listen to him as long as needed if there was a chance to get rid of the apartment. She agreed with Karl that the painting was good and indeed exciting, and yes, it certainly gave her a special feeling when she looked at it. However, she had to admit to herself that she would definitely prefer not to buy it back.

Prince was pleased to see everybody at the Art Society meeting. It was always nice when there were visitors. He had personally greeted each one of them and received a few pats and claps.

He sat on his mat and looked at all the visitors in the study. There they were standing around looking at the walls. Humans were really funny animals. The boss and others kept looking at that smelly thing with the cat shit on it. He knew that humans had no sense of smell. But the ones with the longer hair had put something that smelt of flowers on themselves, maybe to disguise themselves.

He moved over to the group and walked around behind them. For some reason which he had never understood, humans did not like him making close up smell identifications. So at about a half metre's distance he made a smell identification of each visitor. One or two people turned round and there was a little laughter, but he ignored it.

At his nose level all the human smells were there – he could identify each and every one of them. And the flower smelling stuff, which they must have put on to disguise themselves, was in altogether the wrong place – up around their necks and ears. Up there it was not going to disguise anything.

He looked at them again, just standing around wagging their front paws sometimes. They were completely insensitive, not really alive – not what would be classed as alive in the animal world.

Prince went back to his mat to have a sit down and a think. Yes, not really alive. He thought about how it was in the mornings. Humans just flung themselves out of the door and disappeared. When he went out he checked the air to see how the world was smell-wise, then tested the grass, investigated any interesting corners of the garden, and had a look through the gate to see if there were any pals around and suchlike. Prince felt pleased with himself. He knew he had solved life's mystery.

Thinking made his ears stand up, and then the muscles on top of his head started to ache. Oh, rats to it! He got up and trotted through the French windows into the garden and started to play with his old half football, throwing it into the air and then pouncing on it. The members of the Art Society saw him through the windows.

"Look at that crazy dog," someone said, and they laughed.

Prince paused and looked back at them.

"Not really alive," he thought, and continued to have fun with his old half football. He was a very happy dog.

When the Art Society meeting concluded, Karl and his wife said goodbye to their guests standing in the house drive. Karl's mind was in turmoil; there was a real possibility of getting rid of the Bollock painting, but it was going to be somewhat tricky looking at the apartment and not buying it. However, it was very good to know that he had one satisfied customer. But what was Sam Jenkins doing? He could have sold the apartment for a higher price. He really must have a word with Sam Jenkins. Karl shook hands with the minister and promised to go to church, possibly the next day.

Jack drove their hire car home. His mind was also in a turmoil; his pictures were indeed appreciated, and they did have an effect on people. He had to admit that none of them had ever had such an effect on him when he had looked at them. But now he had met a man who had bought one, and he had listened to the man's comments with his own ears. It was indeed very satisfying but he did not understand it. It was a mystery.

Monica was very happy. Think, to be married to such a gifted artist, probably a genius – yes, a genius! And a real chance of getting rid of the apartment.

CHAPTER 7

Over the telephone it was arranged that Karl would visit Jack and Monica at their apartment on the next Friday. Karl arrived on time, complete with certificates from Algernon St. John Villiers that the picture was a genuine Bullock, and a bill of sale for the same, that Karl had adjusted with the help of a scanner and computer to raise the price that he had bought it for by twenty percent.

Monica had prepared the apartment to the best of her abilities. The whole place was spotless, flowers had been bought and placed in strategic places, the kitchen tops which were marked and scratched were scrubbed and bleached with chlorine. She had rehearsed her sales patter at least twenty times per day before Karl's arrival. Jack had prepared his sales patter by adding seven percent to the purchase price of the apartment, to cover the extra costs that had been involved, such as new air conditioning units and so on.

Karl found the apartment to be both acceptable and indeed attractive. It was two and a half years since he had last visited it. The flowers gave it a pleasant atmosphere and the late night noise was not apparent in the afternoon. The sea view from the balcony was always a positive feature for any home.

They went out for a meal at a local Italian restaurant. Over two bottles of wine, one rosé and one red, it was agreed that the painting and the apartment could be bought, however Jack insisted that they sleep on it before deciding. He had a clear suspicion that the purchase price of the painting that Karl had stated was incorrect. Karl, of course, knew that the purchase price stated by Jack was too high by about seven percent. He thanked himself that he had stated a slightly higher price for the painting.

The next day Jack telephoned his agent and also Algernon St. John Villiers, whom he had met twice earlier. His suspicions were confirmed when he found that Karl had indeed raised the price of the picture by twenty percent.

"We will offer him just the price he paid," said Monica, "and see what he says. I'll bet he will take it – it can be a slow business selling pictures."

Karl had already decided that he would offer to buy the apartment for exactly the same price that Jack had paid if need be. He knew it could be a slow business selling an apartment.

A telephone conversation confirmed their offers. Karl drew breath in through his teeth when he heard Jack's offer, but OK, he would get rid of the Bûllock and he would get his money back. Jack and Monica were so pleased to get their money back for their apartment – in truth they would have taken an even lower price.

Karl's lawyer made out contracts for the purchases, and within a week they were signed and monies paid. Jack and Monica could live in the apartment until the end of the month.

After another week the painting arrived at the apartment building on a hired delivery truck. It was now repacked in the original crate in which it had been sent from London. Jack and the delivery man had difficulty moving it into the lift to transport it to the first floor of the apartment. They had some physical help and a great deal of unhelpful advice from the doorman. It cost Jack twenty dollars in tips.

They propped the case against the wall in the lounge. The Bullock had come home.

"I'd like to look at it again," said Jack. "I'll open the packing case tomorrow."

Opening the packing case was not so easy, Jack tried to prise the front off using his largest screwdriver. However that was no good, and he had to go and find a hardware store to buy a crowbar.

"This should do it," he said, and put in an extra effort to open the front. The bottom of the packing case was on the carpet, and suddenly the carpet moved over the polished floor. The top of the packing case slid down the wall. It tore the wallpaper.

"Oh, bollocks."

The damage to the wallpaper was severe: three scratches, one nearly a metre long, and a large triangle of paper torn free.

"Just what we didn't want to happen," was Monica's comment.

"We must fix that before we leave."

Jack continued to remove the front with the packing case flat on the floor. Finally he completed the job, and lifted up the painting in its linen covering. He removed the linen and propped the uncovered painting against the wall.

Monica and Jack stared at it.

"It doesn't look so very impressive. It's something of a

mystery why people buy them," Jack admitted.

"Oh, but it is quite special, and there are many other people who think so too," Monica replied.

Jack walked nearer to the painting and discovered that some of the asphalt from the top edge of the painting had smeared off onto the wallpaper.

"Oh, look at that. I think we will have to repaper the whole room."

"You have a black mark on your shirt too," said Monica.

Jack looked down and found that he had an asphalt mark under his right arm. On his new Hawaiian shirt too. He changed his shirt, and then rang DHL to check how much it would cost to send the painting back to Sweden.

"Do you know it is going to cost about fifteen thousand kronor to send this back. I can paint another for a fifth of that money."

Monica pursed her lips, Jack was a great artist but what he said was true. Monica had an instinctive economy bred from her childhood.

"What do you want to do?"

Jack looked at the painting again and he saw a crack at the top edge of the asphalted turd.

"We can dump this and I'll paint another one when we get back to Sweden."

Jack went over to the drinks cabinet and poured himself a large whisky. Monica said she would like a gin and lime of the same size.

When the whisky was finished Jack went over to the painting and, putting it on the floor, tried to fold it in half. It was not so easy but Monica helped by standing on one edge.

The steel was tough, but with effort the picture was bent almost double.

"We can make it flat by jumping on it."

Jack jumped up and down on the painting and Monica joined in to help, and after a while the two halves were almost touching.

Suddenly there was a loud knocking at their door. It was the neighbour from the floor below who had come to complain about the noise.

Jack apologised and promised that the noise would never occur again.

"We must get rid of this without anybody ever knowing about it or about you getting rid of it," stated Monica.

"We will be classed as idiots paying fifty-two thousand dollars for a work of art and then throwing it away. Also it might affect the value of your paintings in the future."

"OK, I'll fix that," said Jack.

The picture had left a couple of asphalt marks on the floor after the folding efforts.

Jack remembered that there was a building site nearby with waste skips.

"I can throw it into a waste skip this evening and nobody will know anything about it."

In the evening Jack put some newspaper around the edges of the folded painting, tucked it under his arm and set off. The waste skips were there but they were on a building site, which was surrounded by a fence with a barbed wire top. Jack walked along the front and then saw that there was a side street with skips just inside the fence. The side street was badly lit – perfect. He walked up until he was opposite a skip, put the painting into his right hand and, like a shot putter, heaved it over the fence.

"That's it," and Jack turned, and there was a loud crash as the painting landed in the container, plus some sounds of broken glass.

Jack started to walk back down the side street.

"You stop there."

Jack started to hurry.

"You stop there or I'll shoot."

"Oh God, people have guns here." Jack froze and looked at where the voice had come from. A large black man in a blue uniform was approaching on the inside of the wire.

"You can't throw your old plates and auto parts in here. Just you wait right there until the police arrive."

"The police?"

"I pressed the alarm when I heard the noise and saw you."

"The alarm?"

Jack stared at the man on the other side of the fence.

"It was only a piece of steel plate."

"Now listen, man, you can't throw any old steel anything in here."

After a minute Jack saw, out of the corner of his eye, the blue and red flashing lights of a police car as it pulled up at the end of the side street.

Two large policemen got out and walked up the street. They got larger as they approached.

"And what are you doing?"

"He's throwing away bits of plate and auto parts into our skips," answered the uniformed guard.

"Did you do that? You just come with us."

Jack looked up at the policemen and made some sort of noise as he followed along between them. They put one hand on top of his head as they guided him into the back seat of the police car – just as in the films, Jack thought. Jack looked down to check that he had not wet himself. No, that was OK at least.

"We'll take you to the station to get your name and details," said the officer sitting next to Jack.

Jack was silent. He had nothing to say. Where would this end?

When they reached the police station after ten minutes, Jack filled in his name and address at the desk.

"We're real busy just now. You'll have to wait in a cell."

The cell door closed behind a very silent Jack. He sat on the edge of the plastic covered bunk. How had he come to this? What bad luck!

A drunken Mexican signalled to him from the opposite cell.

"Ye're doin good, you'fer coke."

Jack could only shake his head, and he smelled the alcohol in the air. When would he get out? What if Monica could see him now.

However within half an hour an officer came and opened the cell door. "Come along, we'll see about you."

Jack followed with him into another simple white room with a table and chairs.

What to say? He knew instinctively that it was best to be honest and just tell the straightforward truth. His mother had told him that.

The policeman sitting opposite Jack confirmed his name and address, and asked why he had thrown old car parts into the building company's skip.

Jack told his tale, how he was an artist Jack Bullock, and how he had bought one of his own pictures back again, and paid fifty-two thousand dollars for it. Then he and his wife had looked at the picture and then decided that they did not want it. The most sensible course of action (bearing in mind the transport costs and packaging) was simply to get rid of it, and that is why he threw it into the skip.

Jack looked up. The police officer was just staring at him. The policeman then turned his gaze to the ceiling. Another officer came into the room.

"Take this guy away, he's not on our planet but he seems harmless. Tell him he must pay forty-eight dollars for spreading litter. Show him the door and tell him we don't want to see him again."

Jack just sat there.

"You're free to go, but you must pay forty-eight dollars. Follow the officer."

Jack made a noise and followed the officer, paid his forty-eight dollars using his credit card, and was then shown the door.

Outside Jack looked around; he had not been in this area before. He could see the high buildings of the shopping centre. It would take some time to walk there and find his apartment by the shore. He looked around – no taxis either. He could go back in the station and ask them to order a taxi . No, he didn't want to go back in there again.

After an hour and a half he walked back into his apartment.

"Heavens, where have you been? The pizza I bought you has been in the oven for hours."

"Oh, just sit down and I'll tell you all about it," Jack replied.

At the end of the month Jack and Monica had sold their furniture, and re-wallpapered the lounge. They had booked business class tickets on SAS for the return journey. After take-off Monica looked out of the window and saw the dried landscape of the southern United States.

"Well, that's the end of this chapter," said Jack. "We were quite lucky selling the apartment, but it's still something of a mystery to me about why people like my paintings."

"Oh, just forget about that. You have your name as an artist now, that's the main thing. Think of the money and have some fun doing the paintings. We can use an upturned stool to make the round marks, and a long brush to make other marks. Also we can make the paintings a bit different – throw sand and pebbles on them (they'll stick in the asphalt) and what about some wavy lines in different colours?" Monica replied.

"Sounds sensible," and then Jack smiled. "And it does help thinking about the money."

SCHOOL DAYS

My parents registered me at St. Peters Church School and I started there in 1944 when I was seven years old. The school had a good reputation and my parents hoped that I would pass my 11-plus exam.

My first teacher there was an unmarried lady called Miss Roberts. She was about forty-five years old. There were about forty-three children in the class. As children we all knew with a natural instinct that Miss Roberts must be treated with care. She had an uncertain temperament, and could be given over to sudden fits of anger.

Barry Humphrey sat at the back of the class. He had a tendency to be restless and sometimes talk to the other boys around him. These days he would possibly be classified as a boy with ADHD, autism, or some form of hyperactivity. One day Barry was even more talkative than usual and Miss Roberts was in an angry mood.

"Come out to the front, Barry Humphrey."

Barry came to the front of the class and Miss Roberts took hold of a large strap, grabbed hold of Barry's hand and gave him a real whack. Barry winced but did not cry – he was used to the strap and was quite tough for a little boy.

Then Miss Roberts pushed Barry to get him out of the way

and back to his seat. The push took Barry by surprise. He stumbled and fell forward and his head hit the edge of the front desk. The result was a cut on the top of his forehead which started to bleed.

Miss Robert's lips were a thin line as she took out a handkerchief and pressed it over the cut and told Barry to hold it there. She left the classroom to look for the first aid kit in the headmaster's office. She returned with this but there were no large Elastoplasts, just some smaller ones. She used some of these and a piece of lint dressing to cover Barry's cut. However, it could be seen that a little blood ran from under the lint.

At twelve o'clock it was dinner time. There were trestle tables set up in the assembly hall. The food was delivered by an old van from a kitchen somewhere in the town.

Dinner time was greeted with limited enthusiasm by the pupils.

Usually the dinner was 'something' and mashed potatoes. The 'something' could be meat with odd tubes protruding from it. Sometimes there was rissole. Rissole had another name used by the pupil's parents, which sounded somewhat similar. This was followed by semolina pudding.

The mashed potatoes contained little brown patches – quite acceptable. But sometimes there were black pieces. Many young people have good short sight.

Suddenly there was a shout, "There's a piece of a beetle in my potatoes."

A beetle's wing cover had been detected. A little iridescence from this black part showed this to be true. Other pupils on that table stretched forward to see. They confirmed the find. A teacher, Mrs Harrison, approached, with glasses on the end of her nose. She looked at it picked up on the end of another boy's knife.

"That's just a little bit of soot from the kitchen."

Small voices claimed that it was part of a beetle.

Mrs Harrison told them to be quiet and eat all their food.

"You'd be pleased with this food if you lived in China or India."

These boys wished they were in China or India.

All around the hall other boys checked out their mashed potatoes for black pieces. Several were found, and the dinner took ten minutes extra time.

At dinner next day, mashed potatoes were checked again for black pieces. One black piece was found with a beetle's head and two antennae attached. Mrs Harrison and the other teachers carried out an inspection but then had to admit that it was part of a beetle.

They said that the boys did not have to eat their mashed potatoes, and that the kitchen would be told about it.

There were very few black pieces in the potatoes in future, however a grim regime was introduced into the dinner hall. All of the dinners must be eaten by the boys. It was grim for such unappetising food.

Barry and the other boys struggled to eat their dinners – sometimes Barry's comments could be heard.

After the dinner break it was more lessons and then a playtime break.

When the playtime break was finished and Barry returned to the classroom, it could be seen that the cut on his forehead was bleeding steadily under the lint bandage.

Miss Roberts put on new Elastoplasts plus more lint and tore her handkerchief in half and used that too.

When school finished at four o'clock, everyone piled out and went to wait for buses home. While I and others were waiting for a number four bus, we saw Miss Roberts cycle past. That was unusual for she never usually went that way. We looked at Barry who was also waiting for a number four bus.

"Maybe she's cycling home to your house Barry," somebody said.

Yes! It had to be true.

The bus came soon after, and we piled on board and rushed upstairs in spite of shouts from the conductress. Seats at the front were filled immediately and everyone stared through the front windows trying to see Miss Roberts on her bicycle. After a couple of minutes Miss Roberts came into sight, and excitement mounted. But the bus had to stop for passengers and Miss Roberts disappeared again. The bus started off and the road went downhill under the railway bridge and then there was a steep hill up the other side. Miss Roberts came into sight and was overtaken on the steep hill section. All the boys rushed to the rear windows. There was so much noise on the top floor that the conductress rushed up stairs and demanded that everyone must sit down and remain seated otherwise we would be thrown off the bus.

The bus stopped again at Ox-bridge school, where there were many children waiting, and Miss Roberts peddled past. Boys by the windows reported that she was straining hard as she peddled.

"She's trying to get to your house before you, Barry," somebody shouted.

There was quite a delay for the bus at Ox-bridge school and Miss Roberts had completely disappeared when the bus started off again. We boys made an effort to move quietly to the front seats. However, we were not so quiet since there was a struggle to get a place because there was a limited number of front seats. The conductress appeared at the top of the stairs again and demanded quiet. The journey continued and the bus made two more stops and Miss Roberts was still out of sight.

Then there was a long uphill section and Miss Roberts came into sight.

Excitement mounted on the top floor of the bus. Then there was a downhill section as the road passed under another railway bridge. Miss Roberts stayed ahead and made a little distance, but then came a long hill up on the other side and

Miss Roberts was overtaken. Boys rushed for the rear window to look at Miss Roberts struggling up the hill. The conductress came up the stairs and shouted that we boys must get off the bus.

The bus made an unscheduled stop at the top of the hill. A bang could be heard as the driver slammed his door shut after he had climbed out of his cabin. He came upstairs and said it was impossible to drive with all the noise coming from the top floor.

The driver and the conductress said all of us boys must get off. Very fortunately some lady passengers spoke up for us in our defence. They said we had paid for the ride and it was possible for us to sit still – and they would see to it. They had begun to understand that the lady on the bicycle was a teacher from our school and they thought it was rather amusing that we were following her. Two were aunts to us boys.

In the meantime, Miss Roberts cycled past unnoticed.

So we stayed on board and the driver returned to his seat, and the bus set off again. But Miss Roberts had completely disappeared.

The bus made two more stops, and then we all got off at Barry Humphrey's stop. We hurried to Barry's house. As we turned the corner we could see Miss Robert's bicycle parked against the edge of the pavement.

Barry walked into his house with a shout of, "Hello!" We came in behind him.

Miss Roberts was sitting in the kitchen drinking a cup of tea. She looked totally different to the person we knew in school.

Barry's mother was smoking a cigarette and was saying

that Barry often got into trouble and got cuts and scrapes. She got up and looked at the cut on Barry's head. Barry said it was all right, and Barry's mother promptly forgot all about it.

Miss Roberts said we were all good boys and gave us a big smile. We were all speechless and could only look at each other.

Miss Roberts temper was much better during the rest of the time we were in her class. I and all the other boys were so thankful for that.

For my part, I passed my 11-plus exam, but only at the second attempt.

THE CHOIRBOYS OUTING

In the 1950s, most men in Stockton worked at the ICI chemical plant, or the Malleable Iron and Steel Works. The economy was still depressed after the Second World War, and holidays away from home were seldom.

St. Paul's Church was on the outskirts of the town. The church got by on just sufficient funds; the roof needed repairing but the 'roofing fund' only kept abreast with inflation. Most church work was carried out on a voluntary basis: organising a bazaar or helping at the youth club.

The vicar, Peter Rowan, was pleased to have formed a choir with seventeen of the local youths. He had the idea of a day trip for the choirboys and the voluntary church workers. It would be a trip to Whitby, a fishing town, and there were the ruins of a monastery that could be visited.

The train for Whitby left Stockton station at 9.10 on Saturday morning. Fifteen of the choirboys were there, and also the reliable church helpers. There were ladies Jean and Maureen and a Miss Robinson who taught at the Sunday School. There was Arnold too. He had retired from the Navy, and did many of the running repairs for the church – painting, grass cutting and suchlike.

The train carriages were old-fashioned with separate compartments and no corridor. Each compartment could seat five on each side on bench seats. Peter Rowan, who had been talking to the choirboys, ended up in a compartment with nine of them. The remaining six choirboys took the next compartment. Jean, Maureen, Miss Robinson and Arnold were in the third compartment.

Frederick Peacock was one of the six choirboys in the separate compartment. He was eleven years old. He was rather serious and a little overweight. He would greatly have preferred to be in the compartment with the vicar, but now he was alone with just choirboys. Two of these were Michael and Roger, who were fifteen.

Now, choirboys are not always as well-behaved as one would imagine. Michael had brought some cigarette papers and tobacco. When the train started to move he rolled a cigarette, and he and Roger shared smoking it. There was conversation about dares and bets and fights, and a little about girls. The younger choirboys listened and chimed in occasionally, however Frederick's interests were stamp collecting and playing Monopoly, and he found himself excluded.

Of course, it was best to sit next to the window, but there were only four windows and six boys. The two older boys got the two window seats on the left side, which showed the hills and Rosebury Topping, while those on the right showed the backs of houses. But then they passed an airfield which was on the right side – all moved to that side. There were sometimes two or three boys sitting on each other's knees.

Frederick had decided that sitting in the middle away from the windows was quite acceptable. Then he remembered the packet of Maltesers that his mother had given him, and while others were pushing and shoving he quietly extracted one. Just as he popped it into his mouth he was noticed.

"You've got Maltesers – giv'us one."

The pushing and shoving stopped and all eyes focussed on Frederick.

"You've got your own sweets." Sharing things with a special pal was one thing but sharing with five others was unthinkable – there would be nothing left.

Roger had never eaten a Malteser, but he knew they were good.

"What about Jesus feeding the five thousand? There's only five of us and we only want a little Malteser."

Frederick held on to his packet. Michael had the answer.

"Oh, your scarf. I'll just see if I can send a message to the people in the next compartment."

He grabbed Frederick's scarf from the luggage rack. He

pulled the leather strap holding the window up, let the window slide down, and fed the scarf out of the window. Frederick tried to intervene but was easily blocked by the other boys.

Michael put his head out of the window and looked at the scarf.

"It's not long enough to reach the next compartment."

"Let me look," said Roger, and stuck his head out.

"We'll tie his jersey to it and then it'll just reach."

Frederick had taken off his jersey and it was now on the seat beside him. It was grabbed in spite of his best struggles.

The arm of his jersey was tied to the scarf. The combination was a little longer than the scarf, and the whole lot went out through the window.

"Me' mother says it's always good to… air things," Michael said, and the other boys laughed. Frederick was panic-stricken and tried to grab hold of the scarf. The edge of the flapping jersey was seen by Miss Robinson in the next compartment.

"There's something loose outside," she said. Eyes turned to the window, where the bottom edge of the jersey could be seen.

Arnold pulled the belt and lowered the window of the carriage door. He stuck his head out and squinted into the wind. He saw an arm coming out of the window of the compartment ahead, holding a scarf tied to the jersey. He reached out and caught hold of the jersey and pulled it. Michael's face appeared out of the carriage window beside his arm, and Roger's face behind him. Arnold shouted to ask what on earth he was doing but his words were lost in the wind and the noise of the train. He waved the edge of the jersey and Michael, seeing that he had hold of it, let go. The jersey and scarf flew into Arnold's face. He pulled them in through the window. He told the others that it was Michael and Roger playing the fool, and that they deserved a good hiding. All agreed.

"And which poor lad's jersey is it?" asked Miss Robinson.

Michael pulled his head and arm back into the compartment. He could not resist a cruel joke.

"It slipped out' my hand," he said, turning to Frederick.

Frederick was mortified. Lost his jersey! Tears were not far away. He hated Michael and Roger. He screamed at them telling them what it had cost and demanding to know how it was to be, if he was to be by the sea and it was cold.

The three other younger boys were quiet, and Michael and Roger went quiet too, but they smiled and winked at the younger boys.

The remainder of the journey was passed in more or less silence, although Frederick shared some of his Maltesers with the three younger boys.

With the arrival at Whitby excitement returned; who could see the sea first? Who should be first out of the compartment?

They collected on the platform and Miss Robinson gave Frederick his jersey and scarf back. Roger and Michael were collared by Arnold, who explained to them what happened to people in the Navy when they behaved like "thoughtless little buggers".

The vicar joined in saying this was the last trip they would be coming on. The smile disappeared from their faces, but only for five minutes. Also, they knew their voices were changing and they were tired of being in the choir.

The group paid a short visit to the abbey ruins, walked through Whitby centre, and ended up on the beach. There they ate the sandwiches they had brought with them.

Then there was crab hunting, paddling, and a rough game of football. Michael even had a go at swimming, although the water was cold and there was no warm sun.

During the paddling, in which even the vicar took part, Roger and Michael had to have fun hiding other boys' shoes in the sand. In the excitement Arnold's left shoe was also buried.

Arnold did not need his shoes straight away, but when he did, the left shoe could not be found.

The adults searched diligently. Then the vicar told all the choirboys how serious this was, and everyone searched again. However since people had moved between taking their shoes off and paddling, and then finding a place to sit, it was now difficult to know where to search.

Arnold explained again in the clearest terms and language – with the vicar just out of earshot – what happened to people like Roger and Michael in the Navy. They protested their innocence, saying it was only other boys' shoes they had touched – pointless, since Arnold's shoe was missing. It annoyed Arnold even more. After half an hour it was decided that Arnold should buy a pair of sand shoes at Woolworths. But first he had to get to Woolworths on the High Street. Walking on the sand with one bare foot was not so difficult, but on the roads and on the pavements it was different. All small stones were felt by Arnold's bare foot. He was helped by Miss Robinson; he had a hand on her shoulder and eventually was utilising her as a walking crutch. Luckily it was less than half a mile to Woolworths.

At Woolworths, Arnold's luck ran out again. There were no sand shoes of his size. A pair of flip flops was bought. Roger and Michael kept well out of Arnold's way.

All the adults decided that Roger's and Michael's parents would be asked to pay for a new pair of shoes for Arnold. Roger and Michael's protestations were ignored; they had been a complete nuisance during the whole trip.

They reached Whitby railway station in good time for the return journey. When the train came, Frederick Peacock was right behind the vicar as the train was boarded. He was never going to be in a compartment again with Roger or Michael.

Now, Frederick had drunk a lemonade before getting on the train and had a Coca Cola with him, which he drank as soon as they were on their way. After a while he realised that he needed to have a wee. He should have visited the toilet at

Whitby station, but he had only thought of being close to the vicar.

With time, he realised that things were becoming desperate. He told the vicar.

Now, Peter Rowan was a theoretical man. He asked Frederick if the empty Coca Cola bottle could be used. It did look small, and Frederick said so.

"Right," said Peter Rowan, "I will hold open the door and we will hold on to you tightly and you wee out through the gap."

They got in position and braced themselves. The door was opened. Luckily it opened in the direction of travel, and with the vicar holding Frederick tightly, Frederick had a wee.

Two railway workers were standing beside the railway line as the train crossed Yarm viaduct. They had a shock. They could see a carriage door open, a man apparently trying to shut it, and a small boy almost falling out. The man didn't seem able to get the door shut.

A real emergency! They threw down their tools and ran to the line telephone to ring to Eaglescliffe station.

When the train stopped at Eaglescliffe, the station master and porter were ready. They walked the whole length of the train, opening each carriage door and asking if there was any problem. When they reached the vicar's compartment they asked him if there was any problem.

"Oh no," said Peter Rowan. "No problems here."

It was also obvious to the boys in the compartment that opening the compartment door while the train was travelling was certainly the cause of the problem.

The choirboys noted that absolute truth was not always

necessary, even if you were a vicar.

Miss Robinson met Arnold after the Sunday morning church service and invited him for tea that afternoon.

A DAY TRIP BY AEROPLANE

Henry had a small company making punch tools and profiling machines, and anything else that the customer wanted within his limitations. It was hard work with long hours. Delivery times and the payment of value-added tax were a continual worry.

One of his customers wanted to buy an excenter press with special punch tools from a company in Stuttgart. They asked if he could travel with them to give his opinion on their proposed purchases.

The whole trip would only take one day. The Swedish agents would take everyone to Stuttgart in a private plane, flying from Kalmar. Kalmar was a little more than an hour's drive from Henry's workshop. The customer was important, so he said he would go along for the trip. It would be good to see something different and relax for a day.

There was a twin engine aircraft parked at Kalmar airport. When Henry arrived at the airport building, the two company owners, two sales personnel, and two pilots, were waiting. With friendly greetings all round, they walked out and climbed on board the plane.

After take-off there was general discussion and then one of the salespeople asked Henry if he would like a beer. Great, could just be suitable on a free day. When the beer was almost finished he was asked if he would like a whisky. Very suitable; nothing better than a beer and chaser. Another beer was offered as the first one was finished. Henry started to relax. He did not have to drive and the two owners were having whiskies too. Conversation flowed easily.

Life came into perspective as Henry drank his beer and the whisky. His children were established in their careers, house nearly paid for, and not so long to his pension. Yes, life was really not too bad.

While drinking a third beer it became clear to Henry that a visit to the toilet would shortly be necessary. Looking back down the cabin there was only one small door. It was only for Henry to ask.

He was told that there was no toilet, and the little door that he had pointed to was a luggage locker. What to do?

Did the plane land at Copenhagen or Hamburg?

The answer was "No", and it transpired that the trip to Stuttgart would take just over an hour and a half more.

Henry sat and thought about this for over fifteen minutes, and realised that things were becoming desperate. He asked the salespeople who had given him the drinks, what could be done.

A little discussion resulted and they said they had a solution. They had used this plane several times earlier.

They rooted around in the storage locker.

"There is a rubber tube and funnel here. The rubber tube can be connected to the outside. There is a valve and we open the valve and you pee into the funnel."

This was not the day of relaxation Henry had planned. He got down onto his knees and prepared to pee into the funnel. One of the salesmen held the rubber tube and the second prepared to open the valve.

There were two pilots on the plane. One was a lady. She turned around in her pilot's seat and said that one could absolutely not open any valve to the outside air, since the aircraft would lose cabin pressure. There was great pressure for Henry to have a pee, and so difficult to halt that when it was about to start.

What to do? Some thirty-three centilitre beer bottles were quickly produced. It was obvious that these were not at all of a suitable size. Finally a litre bottle was found. It proved to be of just sufficient size.

When he reached Stuttgart it was difficult for Henry to stand upright because of a dull pain in his bladder area. But the pain passed over with time. The factory they visited was interesting and they had a good lunch in a fine restaurant outside of the city.

Henry decided that common sense would prevail on the return journey. No beer or whisky for him when he was in the little aircraft.

After they had been flying for an hour, conversation was again relaxed and free. The company owners were drinking whisky, and the salespeople were delighted having been told that the purchase had been decided.

The plane was flying on 'auto-pilot'. Suddenly the plane turned sharply upwards. Everyone was pressed down in their seats, those facing backwards fell towards the floor. After a couple of seconds the pilots reacted and switched off the 'auto-pilot' and took over manual control. They pressed the nose of the plane downwards.

People on the floor found themselves in the air, and those who had been sitting were also in the air, with hands grasping beneath them trying to find their seats. The whisky from one of the company owners was dripping from the roof.

Henry managed to look towards the pilot's compartment. He could see straight through the cockpit and through the windscreen he could see the lights of a small town. The plane was pointing almost vertically downwards. What does one think about at such a time? Henry could only think that he was in a small private aeroplane and there was absolutely nothing that he could do about it now.

Thankfully the pilots soon had the plane under control. They flew home with the 'auto-pilot' switched off, and landed safely at Kalmar. The salesmen brought all the bags out of the plane and put them on the tarmac. Everyone picked up their bags – but where was Henry's brief case?

They went to the airport building to say their goodbyes. But still Henry's brief case was missing. Then he found it – the lady pilot had it in her hand as she was walking back towards the aircraft. He ran after her and took it from her. She did not know that she had had it in her hand all the time after they had landed.

It had not been the relaxing day trip that Henry had hoped for, but at least he was still alive. However, Henry knew that he would never travel by small private aeroplane again; he would only fly on public airlines, which have such an excellent safety record. Those aircraft also have toilets.

FIRST JOB

On completing his education Henry started work as an apprentice at Vickers Armstrongs, Elswick works, in Newcastle. Vickers Armstrongs engineering factory could make almost anything. They made Centurion tanks at one end, ship's guns in the middle, and huge excenter presses for the motor industry at the other. They also made any kind of gear, hydraulic gear boxes, shell casings, and any other engineering parts that anyone could require. This could include many details for the military.

They could also carry out any kind of coating that was required – nickel, chromium, silver, gold or rhodium.

The restroom in the electrocoating area was dirty and untidy with broken chairs and a worn floor. However the teapot had a thick silver coating and there were gold plated teaspoons.

Vickers lay on a site beside the river Tyne. The site was about two miles long, and was over a hundred years old. It had grown in a random manner with a long winding road along the center and machine shops and assembly areas here and there. There was a hierarchy of workers, starting with cleaners and labourers, following all the way through to fitters, machine operators, tool makers and slingers. Slingers were those at the top of the echelon.

These were the men who fastened the lift cables from cranes to large heavy manufactured pieces, many of which could be of odd shapes. A crane would carry these pieces to a new manufacturing area or load them onto a truck. It was such important work because these objects must be lifted evenly, and must absolutely not tip and fall.

The slingers had their own room, quite high up just under the roof. The room had comfortable old chairs and a sofa, and there were magazines and paperbacks lying around. Here, they could wait until a telephone called them into action. Vickers was such an old factory that this room was unknown to the factory managers. The slinger's room had a small slit window. From this window managers could occasionally be seen as they walked by on the road outside. Occasionally the managers looked up towards the window certainly wondering which room was up there, and were there any people behind the window.

Transport within the factory was difficult. There were older men, some of whom had perhaps been injured earlier while working at the factory, who pulled little trucks with cast iron wheels. These trucks carried small manufactured goods from one area to another, for example, from a milling shop to assembly etc. Larger objects were transported on railway trucks pulled by an old steam engine, which moved along the center length of the factory. Very heavy objects from the machine shops or the press or gun assembly areas were moved on a flat sixty-two wheel wagon, which was pushed by a Sherman tank which had had its turret removed.

'Time and Motion' men, or 'T and M' men as they were called, were not allowed into the factory, as a rule insisted on by the trade unions. Much of the work for the men at Vickers was routine and repetitive. For people doing these routine jobs, then to have extra instructions from the 'T and M' men as to exactly in which order these jobs should be carried out, could be soul destroying.

However the management of Vickers Armstrongs wished to have the viewpoints of 'Time and Motion' experts, and to modernise Vickers. Two 'T and M' men were shown in secret around the factory. This was a time when forklift trucks were becoming common. The 'T and M' men were quite shocked by Vickers internal transport system.

There was a hundred and fifty meter long tunnel along the center of the factory. The two 'T and M' men were in this tunnel when there was a loud rumbling noise. The end of the tunnel became dark as the Sherman tank, pushing a very heavy load, entered. The tunnel was not wide and the two 'T and M' men were pushed into an alcove as the tank and wagon rumbled past. Quite frightening with thought to the enormous load being moved. It was some time before the exhaust smoke cleared.

It was said that the 'T and M' men came to the conclusion that Vickers would require a great deal of reorganisation. They had limited access, and as such it was impossibly difficult for them to help.

The apprentice school was run by Howard Thomlinson. He had been an active trade union member and amongst his responsibilities had been the welfare of workers in number twenty-nine workshop. He had successfully negotiated for new toilets to be installed there. Number twenty-one workshop also had very bad toilets and he had taken that up for discussion. The management then regarded him as a complete nuisance and gave him the job running the apprentice school.

The apprentice school boys were sixteen to eighteen years old. The first impression on entering the apprentice school was surprise and wonder – how could these untidy, somewhat scruffy boys turn into the reliable, stable men who would build the engineering products and run the machines at Vickers?

All the apprentices had to learn how to operate a lathe. There was a complete row of small lathes for the apprentices. Learning to work a lathe was popular with the boys. Pieces could be made for their bicycles, or simple pieces for a car. Of course, it was intensive work operating a lathe. This gave the opportunity for tricks to be played. A favourite trick was to pour white water – used to cool metal when it was in the lathe – into somebody's back pocket as they worked on their lathe. After a couple of minutes the wet feeling would be noticed at the back of the boy's trousers, but by then the culprit had disappeared. It was great fun for boys watching nearby, waiting to see when the wet feeling would be detected, and the reaction of the victim.

There was a little Ford van used by Vickers for internal deliveries within the factory and for transport to a sister factory a little further away down the Scotswood Road. The apprentices were sometimes given the job of cleaning the van and checking the oil and water levels.

There was a windscreen washer with plastic pipes connected to a little hand operated pump, which the driver used to send water to spray nozzles directing cleaning water to the windscreen.

The apprentices disconnected the plastic pipes and directed the pumped water via its plastic pipe under the steering wheel in the direction of the crutch of the van driver. When it rained and the windscreen washer was used, then the helpful cleaning spray of water ended up on the crutch of the driver's trousers.

The first driver using the van when it rained was an older man. He was visiting the Scotswood tractor works; a simple job to deliver machined pieces to the tractor production. The windscreen cleaning pump was operated. Nothing happened. More pumping resulted with increasing irritation. Nothing. He gave up using the pump, but then there was an increasingly wet feeling as the water soaked through the crutch of his boiler suit, through his trousers and through his underpants.

Of course, there was laughter when he delivered his machined details. Not what an older man wanted. Queries as to how often he wet himself were not appreciated.

The windscreen washer pump had its plastic pipes

reconnected again. Could it just have been an accident?

The apprentices serviced the van again and the same trick was tried with the windscreen washer pump. The next time the driver was a foreman on his way to a meeting with the managers at the tractor plant. Considerable annoyance resulted.

After this it was decided that the apprentices were responsible. Who exactly was responsible was never determined however the apprentices never serviced the van again.

The apprentices brought sandwiches from home for lunch. One apprentice who came from a poorer background, secretly and quietly stole another boy's sandwiches. The thief was probably very hungry and certainly hadn't had any breakfast. He was rather short for his age but was energetic.

The other apprentices knew who had stolen the sandwiches and put a piece of asbestos on the steam pipe running along the top of a wall at the back of the apprentice hall.

"Bet you cannot jump up and catch hold of this pipe," someone shouted, as the thief made his way up the room.

One of the apprentices was hanging from the steam pipe with his hands on the asbestos. The thief made a great effort, and jumped up and managed to get his hands onto the pipe. His hands were burned and were uncomfortable for a week. He never stole any sandwiches again. However he did become a very reliable and honest employee.

After the Second World War, having a motor car was a golden goal for most families. Many pre-war cars were kept running by parts and components made at Vickers.

There were Austin 7s with klaxons from a Centurion tank,

an old Jowett car with stainless steel running boards, and a pre-war Vauxhall with magnificent newly-chromed front bumper and hub caps, owned by a man in the plating shop. The plating shop had earlier plated bumpers for Rolls Royce and the Vauxhall's details were in the same class.

There was a car club at Vickers, and the secretary and organiser was Howard Thomlinson. This club had agreements with businesses around Newcastle whereby club members could get a discount on parts such as clutches, brake linings, tyres, etc. Howard Thomlinson had one of the best cars in the club, a post war Ford Consul which he had bought second hand from the Vickers company. This Ford Consul was such a good buy, having always been serviced, and it had modern hydraulic brakes and a heater.

Each year there was a trip organised by the Vickers car club to visit the Barrow-in-Furness works on the other side of the Pennine hills. This was a popular trip for the car club members. It was an interesting trip over the Pennines, and many people had friends in Barrow-in-Furness from earlier trips there.

The day began at eight o'clock from Scotswood Road in Elswick. It was a test of reliability for the member's cars. Most of the cars were pre-war models, and many hours of work renovating these cars were to be put to the test. Each owner took a personal pride in his restoration and the upkeep of his treasured vehicle. It wasn't unusual for a pre-war M.G. Sports to be able to keep up with a post-war Jowett Javelin.

Howard Thomlinson had the privilege of leading the way in his Ford Consul. These were the days before drinking and driving laws had come into operation, and after a couple of hours everyone could stop and meet at a pub at the top of the Pennines. The pub was used each year. There was a lovely view if one sat outside and there was good food and beer. After refreshments and in good spirits, the journey continued. After another hour and a half of driving the Vickers shipbuilding works at Barrow were reached.

There was always something of interest to be seen, ships under construction, ships being fitted out, and an interesting hour and half was spent.

This was followed by lunch at the Palace Hotel where friendships were renewed over beer or perhaps a glass of whisky. Then it was time for the return trip before evening closed in. It was decided that the return trip should be slightly quicker, taking the route through Darlington and following the A1 up to Newcastle. There was a fast downhill road after

Whernside to join the main road to Darlington. Howard Thomlinson was in front in his Ford Consul and certainly going a little too fast. Other old cars were doing their best to keep up. Then the T-junction to the main road to Darlington appeared quite suddenly. Howard Thomlinson could stop in time with his modern car with hydraulic brakes. The car behind him just managed to stop, but further back it was chaos.

A much loved pre-war Jowett drove into the rear of a Beatle Back Riley. This was a great pity since the Riley was in beautiful condition and had been a family's proud possession for many years. A three wheel Morgan ended up with its motor under the back of a Vauxhall tourer. Morris 12s and Austin 10s were locked with their bumpers. Two Austin 7s ran into each other and then into a Singer which collided with a Hillman.

There was an interval which saved many, when a large touring Humber made a supreme sacrifice and swung off the road. It bounced over a ditch and ploughed its own path for thirty yards through gorse and heather. The Humber was heavily loaded with five passengers who had brought bottles of Newcastle Brown Ale with them to drink on the journey. Flat caps were the standard headwear for the men. Their caps were very flat because they impacted the roof of the Humber three or four times as it charged forward. The man in the passenger seat was George Willis, the sixty-two year old foreman from twenty-nine workshop, renowned throughout Vickers for his irritability and short temper. He lost his false teeth as the Humber bounced over the ditch. It was a difficult task to find his teeth on the floor of the car when it finally stopped. There was no hand torch available. He was helped by colleagues using lighted matches for illumination, however with car doors open the matches blew out easily, and this did little to calm George's irritability. George's comments on the situation cannot be printed and must be imagined.

Cars behind the Humber managed to stop.

The day was ruined. The euphoria of lunch and drinks with companions at the Palace Hotel disappeared, and was replaced by panic, anxiety and urgent problems.

There was the problem of which cars were in a fit state to continue and could make the journey home. Cars were pulled apart manually, however this was sometimes difficult because they were on a hill.

The touring Humber needed to be rescued using both a Ferguson tractor and a Fordson Major tractor. Unfortunately the front axle had twisted out of position and it had to be towed to a local garage by the Fordson tractor.

About three quarters of the cars could make it home, perhaps not at full speed and with damage clearly visible. These cars were of course overloaded with extra passengers.

But after the initial shock the question arose of whose fault it was. Who had been driving too fast and who had braked without warning. Clearly many had been driving too fast and many had braked without warning.

But one answer was clear: Howard Thomlinson had been driving too fast with little thought for people with older cars behind him. No consideration had been given to the fact that some of these cars might have rod or cable brakes. Not only that, but Howard Thomlinson had started to drive home again before all the chaos and trouble behind him had been fully cleared up.

The car club members collected money to pay for garage repairs to the cars, in best working men's fashion. Other repairs to metal and paintwork were done by the members themselves. At the Vickers factory in Newcastle the following week, Howard Thomlinson was promptly voted out as organiser and secretary of the car club.

AT SEA

Henry hoped that going to sea as an engineer would be an interesting experience. In 1960 there was a risk of being called up for National Service, but this could be avoided if one was a seagoing engineer. He signed on to work as a junior engineer on a twenty-five thousand ton ore carrier.

The ship was driven by a huge six cylinder Sulzer diesel engine. This engine drove the single propeller directly via a half meter diameter axle. The engine was about three storeys high and it was set to run at a steady speed by a senior engineer. The captain or officers on the bridge sent a signal by telegraph to the engine room as to the speed required.

There was a little leakage of oil from each cylinder of the motor and this was collected in cans that hung on the side of the motor. These needed to be emptied every half hour. The cooling water from the motor went through heat exchangers which used seawater as a coolant, and the flow of sea water had to be adjusted every hour or so.

There were masses of pipes in the engine room and it was necessary to know what was flowing through them. It could be a disaster to open a steam pipe by mistake when one needed compressed air.

There were always two people in the engine room – a senior engineer and a junior engineer. Work as a junior engineer was interesting and normally trouble-free. One did simple jobs: emptying the oil that collected in cans on the side of the engine, cleaning centrifuge separators, painting and suchlike, and making tea for the senior engineer.

Henry worked four hours on and eight hours off. On the free eight hours there was time to sleep, and after that lie in the sun on the deck, read or even study. What could be done otherwise during spare time? Well there was alcohol available. A bottle of rum cost eight shillings, a bottle of gin ten shillings and a bottle of whisky twelve shillings. At this time there were twenty shillings to every pound. A fair amount of alcohol was consumed, but normally it did not interfere with work.

One of the journeys was to Monrovia in Liberia. Monrovia looked great from a distance out at sea, with white buildings and some skyscrapers. However there was a smell similar to a hen house as one sailed nearer. Monrovia was not at all impressive when one landed. On walking into town, the white skyscrapers turned out to be very run-down buildings, almost derelict.

When the boat was lying in the harbour one could see sharks in the water. A hook was made in the workshop of the engine room and he tried to fish for them, using pieces of meat from the ship's kitchen as bait. It was of great interest looking at the sharks swimming around the meat, however Henry never caught a shark.

One time Henry saw another ship entering the harbour. It was an old American ship and it was making a steady speed as it approached the quayside. Suddenly one could see people running quickly up and down the steps to the bridge – something was wrong. It was soon apparent that the ship's engine had fastened in forward speed, and the steering was not functioning correctly. The ship carried straight on and drove into the quayside. When the ship came to a stop the reverse gear was finally engaged and the ship backed out.

The ship was manoeuvred and finally tied up as normal beside the quay. But what had happened to the ship and the quayside?

A day later Henry could go ashore and take a look. The front of the ship had made a cut about one and a half meters deep into the concrete edge of the key. It was a precise cut into the concrete, like a knife into butter. The front of the ship showed no damage whatsoever apart from some marks on the paint.

Sometimes the ship made a trip to Bone in Algeria where iron ore was loaded. At this time there was a civil war in Algeria, but it made no difference to loading the iron ore. One time Henry thought it would be an idea to go ashore and buy a beer at a restaurant. Immediately after stepping ashore he was surrounded by children who wanted money. They followed behind and tried to pick his back pocket. He walked quickly. They disappeared as he neared the town center. There were no restaurants or bars to be found, just an office for Air France.

On the way back to the ship Henry found a French bar on a side street. He opened the door and was faced by a wall of hanging chains. He fiddled around, pushed the chains apart and stuck his head through. Inside there was complete silence; the men sitting at the tables were all staring at him and some were kneeling down. It was clear that the chains were there to stop people throwing bombs into the room. Henry backed out and gave up the idea of buying a beer, and returned to the ship. He fought his way through the children on the return journey and gave them some small change. He was glad to be back on board ship.

There was one occasion when drinking alcohol did interfere with working. At the end of a four hour shift, the rule was to see the next engineers entering the engine room before one left. At the end of Henry's shift the next crew were rather late. He climbed up to the exit door and sat down at the bottom of the door opening to wait. After some minutes the next crew came in. They were fourth engineer Williams and his junior, 'Big' George. They waved to him from the other side of the engine room, and Henry was free to leave.

One could always ask for tea and biscuits if one was hungry. After a couple of hours Henry went into the engine room's rest area to shout up the food delivery lift for tea and biscuits. It was sensible to ask via the engine room, since sometimes the two cooks in the kitchen could be in bad humour at the end of the day, and a request at the kitchen door could result in being threatened by a knife.

Henry saw there was nobody down near the engine, and there was nobody in the restroom either. He looked around. The answer could be found in the shower area. Williams had collapsed in the shower with the water still running over him and 'Big' George was fastened in a toilet cubical with the door jammed against his legs. There was a strong smell of alcohol.

What to do? Henry found another junior engineer and they looked at the huge Sulzer engine. They could empty the overflowing oil, and even alter the cooling water, but they could not alter the motor speed if that was needed.

The ship was charging forward at about fourteen knots, twenty-five thousand tons with its cargo of about eighteen thousand tons of iron ore. They went to look for the third engineer for help. He was not in his cabin or in the canteen area. They went to find the second engineer. This was serious because Williams' and George's drunkenness would have to be reported. However the second engineer could not be found. They had to tell the chief engineer. They went to his cabin. At the door could be heard laughs and music from a gramophone. They knocked on the door and a red face appeared and they were told to get lost. The door was slammed closed again.

They knocked again, and when the door was opened they shouted that there was nobody in the engine room, and that the engineers were drunk. There was a little pause and then a stony silence. Then there were shouts and the chief engineer, the second and the third engineers piled into the corridor. The second engineer fell over with the third engineer on top of him. They picked themselves up and they all rushed down to the engine room. Temperatures were quickly stabilised for the engine. Williams was carried out of the shower and, still unconscious, dumped onto his bed in his cabin. 'Big' George was left sitting on the toilet since nobody could get him out of that cubicle. It was Williams last trip to sea and probably 'Big' George's too.

The ship returned to England and stopped in port several days for unloading. There were two boilers in the engine room which supplied hot water and steam to the ship. One of these boilers was kept running while the ship was in port, and a shore donkeyman was employed to look after the boiler at night.

Henry was cleaning a centrifugal separator when he heard a very large crash. He was quite used to loud noises when hatch covers on the holds were dropped. He turned around only to see a sheet of flame in front of the boiler. There had been an explosion and the door on the front of the boiler had blown open. Burning oil had sprayed out over the wall at the back of the boiler and over the insulation around the oil supply tank fastened higher up on the wall. Fortunately the door of the boiler had flown over the head of the shore donkeyman but his boiler suit had been set alight by the spray of burning oil. He danced around in pain and panic but he thought quickly and managed to turn off the oil supply. Henry tried to clap his boiler suit with rags to put out the flames. The donkeyman managed to get the boiler suit off.

What to do? There was a very large fire extinguisher at the back of the boiler. But there was a long list of instructions printed on the side as to how to get it to operate. Not just that, but the spray hose was tied in place in best seaman fashion, with thick string with tight knots and the ends of the string cut off short. Henry found a small fire extinguisher and turned it upside down and banged the spray-end onto the deck – nothing. Fortunately the captain arrived on the scene, grabbed another fire extinguisher and banged the spray-end very hard onto the deck and got it to work.

Henry and a seaman helped with other fire extinguishers. In the panic they even sprayed each other a little, however that did not matter.

The poor shore donkeyman was taken to hospital and unfortunately his burnt boiler suit was thrown into the river. It had his false teeth in the pocket.

The next day, when Henry went on shore he met the chief engineer and another junior engineer on a little bridge over a channel by the river. The chief asked if anything had happened. Oh! said Henry, a boiler had exploded, there had been a fire in the engine room and a man had been injured. The chief just grunted and pushed past. He said afterwards to the other junior engineer that he was tired of Henry's jokes, and he had a good mind to throw Henry in the river.

He continued on his way but in a few minutes he could see the ship tied alongside the dock with a blackened funnel, and the parked cars of the superintendents from the shipping line and a police car. People had come to investigate the accident.

It was Henry's last trip to sea; he thought that it offered a limited future and there was a possibility of becoming an alcoholic if he continued with such a life.